Inside the NBA
Utah Jazz

Paul Joseph

ABDO & Daughters
PUBLISHING

Published by Abdo & Daughters, 4940 Viking Dr., Suite 622, Edina, MN 55435.

Copyright ©1997 by Abdo Consulting Group, Inc., Pentagon Tower, P.O. Box 36036, Minneapolis, Minnesota 55435. International copyrights reserved in all countries. No part of this book may be reproduced in any form without written permission from the publisher. Printed in the United States.

Edited by Kal Gronvall

Library of Congress Cataloging–in–Publication Data

Joseph, Paul, 1970-
    The Utah Jazz / by Paul Joseph
        p. cm. — (Inside the NBA)
    Includes index.
    Summary: Overviews the history and key personalities of a basketball team that, after a move from New Orleans, has been a consistent winner and Western Conference contender.
    ISBN 1-56239-776-1
    1. Utah Jazz (Basketball team)—History—Juvenile literature.
[1. Utah Jazz (Basketball team)—History. 2. Basketball—History.]
I. Title. II. Series.
GV885.52.U8J67 1997
796.323' 64' 09792—dc21   97-1337
                                                    CIP
                                                    AC

Contents

Utah Jazz

The Utah Jazz began as the New Orleans Jazz in 1974 as an expansion team in the National Basketball Association (NBA). After struggling a decade at the bottom, the Jazz came out in the late 1980s and 1990s as contenders for the Western Conference title. In the 1996-97 season they won the Western Conference, and made their first ever appearance in the NBA Finals.

The original Jazz of New Orleans featured a home-town hero. High-scoring Hall of Famer "Pistol Pete" Maravich was one of the most entertaining players in NBA history. Although he never led his Jazz to championships, fans still came out by the thousands to watch this magician do things with a ball that people had never seen before.

When the franchise relocated to Utah, the team was led by many stars. There was scoring machine Adrian Dantley, big dunker Darrell Griffith, assist king John Stockton, and Karl Malone, a forward with so much power and grace that he has become one of the most dominant stars in the league, picking up the NBA Most Valuable Player (MVP) Award in the 1996-97 season.

Today, point-guard John Stockton is still the floor leader, and Karl Malone is still the go-to guy. Since the two have been together, the Jazz have always contended for the NBA title. Although they have yet to capture their much-deserved championship, they haven't given up.

Facing page: The Utah Jazz' All-Star Karl Malone.

"Pistol Pete"

On March 7, 1974, the New Orleans Jazz became the 18th member of the NBA, in return for a $6.15-million expansion franchise fee. Local businessmen in New Orleans knew there was a need for basketball in their city. They named the team the Jazz in recognition of the city's glorious musical tradition.

The owners' first and biggest move was a trade with the Atlanta Hawks. The Jazz acquired the flashy six-foot, five-inch Maravich. Aaron James was the team's first selection in the NBA Draft, and the Jazz filled out the roster with veterans chosen from other teams in the 1974 NBA Expansion Draft.

The Jazz realized that their expansion team was not likely to post a strong record in the beginning. So the owners opted to bring someone in that the fans would love to see. The obvious choice was local hero Pete Maravich.

Maravich already had the tag "Pistol Pete" when he was in high school because of his from-the-hip shooting style. He could pass, dribble, and shoot like none other. New Orleans fans saw him dominate in college for Louisiana State University (LSU). Maravich finished his college career as the second-highest-scoring player in college history, with 3,667 points, or an incredible 44.2 points per game average! In 28 of those games, he scored 50 points or better, including games of 69 and 66 points.

Maravich then went on to the NBA, where he was drafted by the Atlanta Hawks, third overall in the 1970 NBA Draft. The Hawks inked him to the first-ever million dollar contract. In his four years with Atlanta, "Pistol Pete" put on an impressive performance, averaging 24.3 points and 5.6 assists per game.

Maravich had experienced problems with his Atlanta teammates because of the money he made and his star status. After four straight second-place finishes, the Hawks agreed to trade their star to the new team in the league, the New Orleans Jazz. "Pistol Pete" was excited to be coming home to fans who truly loved him and to a team that really wanted him.

"Pistol Pete" Maravich goes in for a layup.

The New Orleans Jazz

In New Orleans' inaugural season the team hired Scotty Robertson as head coach, and named future Hall of Famer Elgin Baylor as one of Robertson's assistants. What the fans were really excited for was "Pistol Pete" Maravich. People packed the stadium to see him work his magic.

In New Orleans' first NBA regular-season game, the Jazz were dumped by the New York Knicks, 89-74. That first loss was only the beginning. The team lost 10 more games before picking up its first-ever victory over the Portland Trail Blazers. With the Jazz 1-14 on November 17, the team gave up on Robertson and hired Butch Van Breda Kolff to take over the head coaching duties.

The Jazz finished their first season with a 23-59 record and last place in the Central Division.

The only highlight of the year was Maravich. "Pistol Pete" became the team's main attraction and top scoring threat. Maravich was a showman who would shoot the ball from anywhere and everywhere. He never made a simple pass when he could make an entertaining one, so his assists would usually come from behind the back or through his legs. Maravich averaged 21.5 points and 6.2 assists per game. He was the only starter on the team to score more than 12 points per game.

For the New Orleans Jazz, the first year was the beginning of a pattern. Throughout the 1970s the Jazz never made the playoffs. They did show improvement, however.

In the 1975-76 season they climbed one step to fourth place as Maravich's scoring average rose to 25.9, third best in the league. He also was named to the All-NBA First Team.

Maravich's best year as a pro came the following season. "Pistol Pete" took the scoring championship with a 31.1 average, including a 68-point game against the New York Knicks. In 13 of the games he scored 40 points or more. Maravich also led the league in minutes played, and led the Jazz in assists with 5.4 per game. He again was named to the All-NBA First Team.

For the Jazz, the team dropped to 35-47, mainly because they were weak defensively and on the boards. They did, however, stay a notch above the Hawks, finishing in fifth place in their division.

Elgin Baylor Becomes The New Coach

Two months into the 1976-77 season, Elgin Baylor was elevated from assistant coach to head coach. Baylor came back the following year to coach the entire season.

It was another up-and-down season for Baylor and the Jazz. New Orleans finished the 1977-78 season 39-43, occupying the familiar second-to-last position in the Central Division.

In January, the Jazz got hot, winning 10 straight. Then on January 31, Maravich injured his knee making a between-the-legs pass. The team had lost their most potent offensive force, as he appeared in only three more games the rest of the season.

The Jazz did feature newcomer Leonard "Truck" Robinson. Robinson was a muscular, 6-foot, 7-inch, 225-pound forward who crashed the boards with reckless abandonment, and could score too.

Robinson turned in seven 20-rebound games, including a team record of 27 twice. The Truck led the NBA in defensive rebounds, total rebounds, and rebounding average with 15.7 per game. Robinson became the first Jazz player to go over 1,000 rebounds for the season. To top off the incredible season, Robinson also scored 22.7 points per game and was named to the All-NBA First Team.

New Orleans returned to the basement in the 1978-79 season, finishing with a 26-56 record. The Jazz failed to produce a winning month, and won only four road games all season.

Most of the team's problems occurred when Robinson was traded in January. Robinson was by far the most productive player on the team, since Maravich continued to struggle with knee problems. "Pistol Pete" missed the final 21 games of the season. Without Robinson or Maravich, the team was in disarray.

Fans were upset with the play of their Jazz, and financial difficulty led to the sale of the team. By the start of the 1979-80 season there would be a whole new look for the Jazz.

Jazz In Utah?

Big changes happened in 1979-80. The biggest change was the team's move to Salt Lake City, Utah—a city that couldn't be more opposite than New Orleans. Around the league, jokes were made about a team named the Jazz moving to Utah.

The Utah Jazz had a new owner in Larry Miller and a new head coach in Tom Nissalke. They also were moved to a new division, the Midwest Division of the Western Conference.

The most important acquisition was Frank Layden, a portly, colorful individual who would become known as "Mr. Jazz" for the next decade. Layden became the first general manager in Utah and would go on to transform the Jazz into consistent winners and Western Conference contenders.

In another key move before the season, Utah acquired fourth-year guard-forward Adrian Dantley. The 6-foot, 5-inch scoring machine proved to be just what the Jazz needed.

Dantley filled the void left by the high-scoring Maravich, who was waived by the Jazz after failing to come back after knee injuries. After being picked up by the Boston Celtics, Maravich decided that he could never regain his full capabilities and retired. "Pistol Pete" was a five-time All-Star and was inducted into the Hall of Fame in 1986. On January 5, 1988, tragedy struck as Maravich collapsed and died playing a pick-up basketball game. The New Orleans Jazz will always be associated with their exciting, offensive magician, "Pistol Pete" Maravich.

The first year in Utah was much like the ones in New Orleans. The team's record was 24-58, good for last place in their new division. The year was highlighted by Dantley who ranked third in the league in scoring with 28 points per game.

Adrian Dantley
drives toward
the basket.

Layden Takes Over

Although Dantley was an offensive machine, the Jazz still needed another scorer. So with the second pick in the 1980 NBA Draft, Utah selected College Player of the Year Darrell Griffith, from the University of Louisville. Griffith, a quick 6-foot, 4-inch guard, was both a high-flying slam dunker and a deadly shooter.

Griffith and Dantley provided a potent one-two scoring punch as they combined for 51.3 points per game. With the two stars, the team improved slightly to 28-54, good enough to stay out of the basement of the Midwest Division.

13

Dantley made his second consecutive All-Star Game appearance and won the NBA scoring title with an average of 30.7 points per game. Griffith averaged 20.6 points and was named NBA Rookie of the Year.

Utah struggled again in 1981-82, finishing at 25-57. After 20 games Frank Layden left the front office to become head coach of the Jazz. Layden would hold the position until 1988, and in that time he would turn the team into a winner.

Dantley continued to carry the team, scoring 30.3 points per game, third best in the NBA. Rickey Green, a 6-foot, 1-inch guard, finished sixth in the league in steals and seventh in assists.

With the third pick in the 1982 NBA Draft, the Jazz selected another scoring machine in Dominique Wilkins. But Wilkins never suited up for Utah. On September 2, he was traded to Atlanta for John Drew, Freeman Williams, and cash. The Jazz did, however, select Mark Eaton in the fourth round. The 7-foot, 4-inch, 286-pound giant was a much needed force in the middle and had a productive career with the Jazz.

The 1982-83 campaign was not good for the Jazz. Dantley tore ligaments in his right wrist and missed the final 60 games. Without Dantley the team fell to 30-52, its fifth consecutive 50-loss season.

Griffith kept on scoring, leading the Jazz with 22.2 points per game. Green had another productive year, finishing third in the league in assists and second in steals. Newcomer Mark Eaton was second in blocked shots with 275 for the season.

Finally, The Playoffs

The Jazz improved drastically in the 1983-84 season. The turnaround began in the June NBA Draft, when the team selected 6-foot, 11-inch Thurl Bailey of North Carolina State in the first round. They also chose Bobby Hansen in the third round.

After nine consecutive losing seasons, the Jazz broke through with a 45-37 record for their first-ever Midwest Division title. The team was healthy throughout the entire season, with seven players appearing in 80 or more games.

Utah finished December with an 11-2 mark, the best month in franchise history. The team built a 17-game winning streak at home that lifted them to the top of their division.

Dantley was again the star of the team. He became only the fourth player in league history to sink 800 free throws in a season. Dantley was selected to his fourth All-Star Game and finished the season as the NBA scoring champ with a 30.6 average.

The Jazz, however, were not a one-man show. Utah became the first team in history to have four players with NBA statistical crowns. There was Dantley in scoring, Green in steals, Eaton in blocked shots, and Griffith in three-point percentage.

Bailey was a key contributor as a rookie for the Jazz. He was named to the All-Rookie Team, while Dantley, who returned from a wrist injury, was awarded the league's Most Improved Player. In addition, Frank Layden was named NBA Coach of the Year.

After clinching the Midwest Division, the Jazz were on their way to their first-ever post season. They needed five games to get by the Denver Nuggets in the first round. In the Western Conference Semifinals they were upset by the Phoenix Suns in six games. The season, however, was a success for the Jazz, who had now tasted the playoffs for the first time.

John Stockton leaves Golden State Warriors' forward Joe Smith on the floor as he breaks for the basket.

John Who?

In the 1984 NBA Draft, the Jazz stole a player that would go on to be the assist king of the NBA, and put Utah on a winning path for more than a decade. With the 16th pick overall, the Jazz selected little-known 6-foot, 1-inch guard John Stockton of Gonzaga University. People were surprised with the pick, but not the Jazz. They had studied Stockton in college and knew he had great promise. Not even the Jazz dreamed he would end up rewriting the assists' record book.

Mark Eaton continued to develop into a great shot blocker. Eaton was named NBA Defensive Player of the Year, mainly for his record number of blocks. He won the shotblocking title and set an all-time league record for total blocks with 456, and blocks per game with 5.56. On January 18, Eaton set a Jazz record by rejecting 14 shots in one game.

The Jazz played .500 ball throughout the 1984-85 season, finishing with a 41-41 record. Once again they were in the playoffs. The Jazz defeated the Rockets in five games, but then were knocked out by the Nuggets, four games to one, in the Western Conference Semifinals.

With Stockton leading the way for the team on the floor, the Jazz knew they had to get a player who could take his passes and score. In the 1985 NBA Draft they finally found a player who could deliver.

Utah

All-Star and Hall-of-Famer "Pistol Pete" Maravich joined the New Orleans Jazz in their 1974-75 inaugural season as a result of a trade with the Atlanta Hawks.

Adrian Dantley won two NBA scoring titles while playing for the Jazz, one in the 1980-81 season, and the other in the 1983-84 season.

Jazz

John Stockton, who helped lead the Jazz to the 1996-97 NBA Finals, has the most assists in the history of the NBA.

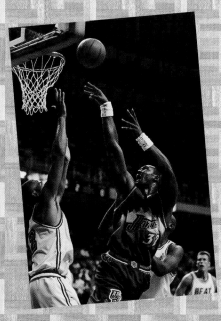

Karl Malone was awarded the NBA MVP in the 1996-97 season after leading the Jazz to 64 wins and a Western Conference Championship.

"The Mailman"

Karl "The Mailman" Malone was selected by the Jazz with the 13th overall pick in the 1985 NBA Draft. The 6-foot, 9-inch, 256-pound Louisiana Tech grad would go on to become one of the best power forwards ever to play the game. The Mailman—a nick-name a sportswriter gave Malone because he always delivers—is a ferocious inside player who loves to run the court.

Malone and Stockton would go on to form the best point-guard-to-power-forward tandem in basketball history. Game after game, quarter after quarter, it was Malone running full steam down the court to a spot where he knew Stockton would get him the ball. Or it was Stockton, slashing and penetrating and dishing off a pass in midair to Malone. It was superb, exciting basketball, and Jazz fans loved it.

In the tandem's first year together they led the Jazz to their second winning season in team history with a 42-40 record. Utah advanced to the postseason but lost in the first round to the up-and-coming Dallas Mavericks.

Dantley still led the way for the Jazz with 29.8 points per game, second in the NBA, in what would be his last season with the Jazz. Eaton was again a shotblocking force and made the All-Defensive First Team. Malone, who averaged 14.9 points and 8.9 rebounds, made the NBA All-Rookie Team.

End Of An Era

Utah continued to build for the future. Prior to the 1986-87 season, the Jazz traded Dantley to the Detroit Pistons for Kelly Tripucka and Kent Benson. The high-scoring era of Adrian Dantley in Utah had come to a close. Malone took over the scoring duties, leading the team with a 21.7 average. John Stockton continued to improve while dishing out 8.2 assists per game.

The Jazz finished with a respectable 44-38 record, good enough to earn the Jazz a fourth consecutive playoff appearance. Utah jumped out to a two-games-to-none lead and looked like they would steal the best-of-five series from the Golden State Warriors. The Jazz, needing only one win, lost three in a row and were bumped from the playoffs.

The 1987-88 Jazz had a strong, young line-up. The team had their best record to date with 47 wins and 35 losses. The team's success focused mainly on their two young stars. Malone was voted to start in the 1988 NBA All-Star Game. He led the Jazz in both scoring (27.7 ppg) and rebounding (12.0 rpg). Stockton broke the single-season record for assists with 1,128 (13.8 per game). Mark Eaton won his fourth shotblocking title, recording 3.71 blocks per game.

In the playoffs, Utah faced Portland in the first round of the 1988 NBA playoffs. The Jazz lost the first game, then swept the next three to advance to the Western Conference Semifinals. Facing the World Champion Los Angeles Lakers, Utah forced the series to seven games before falling by 11 points in the final game.

The Stockton-Malone Era

The 1988-89 season officially began the Stockton-Malone era, and the rest of the league took notice of this great combination. Besides the one-two punch of Stockton and Malone, the team was also the best defensive unit in Jazz history, giving up only 99.7 points per game. The defense was led by the shot blocking of Mark Eaton.

Just 17 games into the season, eighth-year head coach Frank Layden resigned to become the team's president. Assistant coach Jerry Sloan, a former Chicago Bulls All-Star guard, took over the head coaching reigns and guided Utah to a 51-31 record and another Midwest Division title.

Malone, Stockton, and Eaton represented the franchise at the 1989 NBA All-Star Game, where the Mailman earned the MVP Award with 28 points and 9 rebounds. Stockton not only led the league in assists for the second year in a row, but was also the league's steals leader. Malone finished second in the NBA in scoring with a 29.1 points per game average. The Mailman was selected to the All-NBA First Team and finished third in voting for the league's MVP Award. Eaton, who was second in the league in blocked shots and seventh in rebounding, earned his second Defensive Player of the Year Award.

With an excellent regular season, the Jazz were primed to make a run at the NBA Championship. Instead, Utah fell apart in the first round and were upset by the Golden State Warriors.

Utah bounced back in 1989-90 with another franchise-best 55-27 record. The team sprinted out of the gate, winning seven of its first eight games and notching a 19-game home winning streak in the middle of the season.

The team was again led by the Stockton-Malone combo. Malone's 31 points per game ranked second in the league to Michael Jordan, and he set a franchise record for points in a season with 2,540. Stockton broke his own NBA record by dishing out 1,134 assists for an incredible 14.5 per game average.

The Jazz, however sputtered at the end of the year. Utah finished 5-7 in April, and continued to struggle in the postseason. The Jazz were knocked off by the Phoenix Suns in the first round of the playoffs.

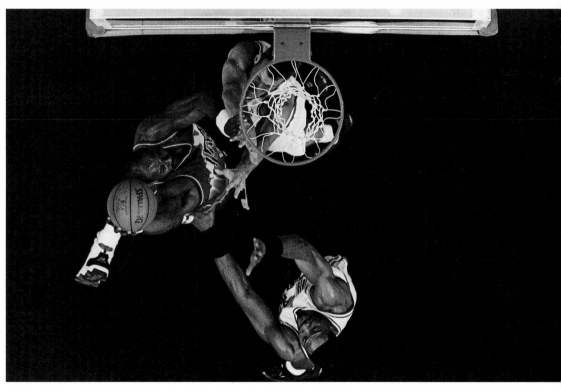

Karl Malone slam dunks the ball for an easy two points.

Another Malone

Recognizing the team's lack of depth, the front office acquired a solid shooting guard in Jeff Malone (no relation to Karl). With Stockton and the two Malones, Utah put together another 50-win season in 1990-91, finishing with a 54-28 record. Stockton once again broke his assists record with 1,164, reaching the 1,000-assist plateau for the fourth consecutive year. Karl Malone had another great year, scoring 29 points and grabbing 11 boards a game.

For the second straight year the Jazz met the Suns in the first round of the playoffs. This time, however, Utah grabbed the series in four games. But that would be it for the Jazz, who were bumped by the Portland Trail Blazers in five games in the second round.

The Jazz had their best season ever in 1991-92. Playing in their new Delta Center, Utah captured the best home record in the league with 37 wins and only 4 losses. They won 55 games and dominated the Midwest Division.

In the playoffs, Utah defeated the Los Angeles Clippers. Then the Jazz roughed-up the Seattle SuperSonics four games to one on their way to their first-ever Western Conference Finals. But Utah met their match as the Portland Trail Blazers won the series in six games.

Stockton and the two Malones led the way in this historic Jazz season. Stockton led the team in assists with 13.7 per game and topped the 1,000-assist plateau for a record fifth consecutive year. The Mailman again finished second in the league in scoring with 28 points per game. Jeff Malone ranked second on the team in scoring with 20.2 points per game.

24

Dynamic Duo

In the 1992-93 season, the Jazz slipped to 47-35 and made a first-round exit from the playoffs, thanks to the Seattle SuperSonics. There were some highlights, however, for the fans of Utah.

Karl Malone and John Stockton played on the 1992 Summer Olympic "Dream Team." The awesome team also featured Michael Jordan, Magic Johnson, and Larry Bird, to name a few. The Dream Team dominated the rest of the world on their way to a gold medal.

The dynamic duo also stole the show in front of their hometown fans at the 1993 NBA All-Star Game. Malone and Stockton shared MVP honors as they led the West to a 135-133 overtime victory at the Delta Center.

During the season, Karl Malone scored his 15,000th point and also became the Jazz's all-time leading rebounder. Eaton blocked his 3,000th career shot, making him only the second player to reach that mark. Stockton won his sixth straight assists title, reaching 8,000 for his career.

The Jazz came back in 1993-94 to post a 53-29 record. It was the same formula of Stockton to Malone. But this year they made a trade that brought in Jeff Hornacek for Jeff Malone. Hornacek, a guard with great passing skills and a sweet jumper, helped the Jazz improve.

In the playoffs the Jazz dumped the San Antonio Spurs in four games. They needed seven games to put away the Nuggets. In the Western Finals, the Houston Rockets and Hakeem Olajuwon were too much for the Jazz, as they were ousted in five quick games.

Best Jazz Teams Ever

The Jazz had as much talent as any other team in the league in 1994-95. They had a great starting five and a deep bench filled with talent and size. The Jazz played like a finely oiled machine on their way to posting 60 wins—the best ever in Jazz history. Malone was excited about Utah's chances in the playoffs, saying it was the best team he had ever been on.

Again it wasn't to be. One of the most talented teams in basketball couldn't get by the first round of the playoffs, losing to the Houston Rockets in five games.

The Jazz bounced back in 1995-96, determined to make a run at the title. Their depth, veteran leadership, and all-around solid team play translated into 55 regular season wins and an excellent postseason.

In the first round, the Jazz slipped by the Portland Trail Blazers. They took the San Antonio Spurs in six games, which gave them a legitimate shot at the NBA Finals. They first would have to get by the Seattle SuperSonics in the Western Finals. The Jazz rallied from a three-games-to-one deficit to tie the series and force a seventh game. The Jazz came within two baskets of making it to their first NBA Finals, losing 90-86.

The Finals

The Utah Jazz came out in the 1996-97 season and continued to be one of the top teams in the NBA. With 64 wins, the Jazz had their best season ever, won the Midwest Division, and had the best record in the West. They had the second-best record in all of the NBA. However, from All-Star break on they were the best.

The 1996-97 team had a well-balanced attack with great play coming from everyone. Greg Ostertag, Bryon Russell, Hornacek, Shandon Anderson, and Greg Foster all played important roles. But once again the season relied heavily on Stockton and Malone. For Malone's outstanding play he was named the NBA's MVP.

The Jazz continued to be the best in the postseason. In the first round against the Los Angeles Clippers, Utah destroyed them in three quick games. In the next round, the Jazz did the same to the other Los Angeles team, the Lakers.

In the Western Conference Finals against the Houston Rockets, the Jazz battled and played hard. In the end Utah prevailed because of the disciplined team play that was instilled by coach Jerry Sloan. But more importantly the dynamic duo were determined to make it to the Finals.

In Utah's first ever NBA Finals, they were matched against one of the greatest teams in NBA history, the Chicago Bulls. The Bulls, led by Michael Jordan, Scottie Pippen, and Dennis Rodman, came out and captured the first two games in Chicago. The determined Jazz didn't give up, though. The Jazz won the next two games in Utah to even the series. Games 5 and 6 were so evenly played that they could have gone either way. Unfortunately, for the Jazz, it went Chicago's way. The Utah Jazz finished their greatest season ever as the NBA's runner-up.

Karl Malone executes a jump shot for two points.

The Clock Is Ticking

The clock is ticking down on the Utah Jazz. With the best duo ever to play the game getting older, the Jazz may have only a few more years before Malone and Stockton retire.

If any two players deserve a championship it is Stockton and Malone, who play with every ounce of energy every time they step onto the court. The two have rewritten the record books, but would gladly give up the records for a championship.

The Jazz franchise struggled through the early days in New Orleans, and lately has seen great teams come up short. One thing is for sure, though: From Maravich to Dantley to Stockton and Malone, Jazz fans have been thoroughly entertained.

Glossary

American Basketball Association (ABA)—A professional basketball league that rivaled the NBA from 1967 to 1976 until it merged with the NBA.

assist—A pass of the ball to the teammate scoring a field goal.

Basketball Association of America (BAA)—A professional basketball league that merged with the NBL to form the NBA.

center—A player who holds the middle position on the court.

championship—The final basketball game or series, to determine the best team.

draft—An event held where NBA teams choose amateur players to be on their team.

expansion team—A newly-formed team that joins an already established league.

fast break—A play that develops quickly down court after a defensive rebound.

field goal—When a player scores two or three points with one shot.

Finals—The championship series of the NBA playoffs.

forward—A player who is part of the front line of offense and defense.

franchise—A team that belongs to an organized league.

free throw—A privilege given a player to score one point by an unhindered throw for goal from within the free-throw circle and behind the free-throw line.

guard—Either of two players who initiate plays from the center of the court.

jump ball—To put the ball in play in the center restraining circle with a jump between two opponents at the beginning of the game, each extra period, or when two opposing players each have control of the ball.

Most Valuable Player (MVP) Award—An award given to the best player in the league, All-Star Game, or NBA Finals.

National Basketball Association (NBA)—A professional basketball league in the United States and Canada, consisting of the Eastern and Western conferences.

National Basketball League (NBL)—A professional basketball league that merged with the BAA to form the NBA.

National Collegiate Athletic Association (NCAA)—The ruling body which oversees all athletic competition at the college level.

personal foul—A player foul which involves contact with an opponent while the ball is alive or after the ball is in the possession of a player for a throw-in.

playoffs—Games played by the best teams after the regular season to determine a champion.

postseason—All the games after the regular season ends; the playoffs.

rebound—To grab and control the ball after a missed shot.

rookie—A first-year player.

Rookie of the Year Award—An award given to the best first-year player in the league.

Sixth Man Award—An award given yearly by the NBA to the best non-starting player.

trade—To exchange a player or players with another team.

Index